CHILDREN OF THE FOREST

FOREST

Elsa Beskow

Floris Books

First published in Swedish under the title *Tomtebobarnen* by Albert Bonniers, Stockholm in 1910
This edition published in 2005 by Floris Books, 15 Harrison Gardens, Edinburgh
Seventh printing 2015
© BonnierCarlsen Förlag, 2007
English version by Alison Sage © Ernest Benn Ltd, 1982
British Library CIP data available
ISBN 978–086315–497–3   Printed in Malaysia

Deep in the forest, under the curling roots of an old pine tree, was a small house. Warm and dry in winter, cool and airy in summer, it was the home of one of the forest people. He lived there with his wife and four children; Tom, Harriet, Sam and Daisy.

Wild strawberries and mushrooms grew by their door and they had all the pots, pans, chairs, beds, tables, knives, forks and spoons they could possibly need. Sheltered under the pine tree branches, they hardly felt the autumn gales and if it rained, the children crept underneath a giant toadstool to keep dry.

All the children wore red-and-white spotted caps. If strangers came into the forest, they curled up, still as stone, for all the world like four red-and-white spotted mushrooms.

But most of the time they were perfectly safe. Then they played at hide-and-seek with the squirrels, who lived upstairs in the tree.

Squirrels are scatty, thoughtless creatures and sometimes they forgot what game they were playing and then the children could catch them. Mostly, they were kind-hearted and often they remembered to bring Harriet a nut or two from their store.

On summer evenings, the children went down to the pool to see their friends the frogs. Buffo, who was big and fat and kind was especially fond of little Daisy and he would always listen to her troubles.

"Renata!" shouted Harriet. "Come and tell us how many insects you've caught." Renata the bat pretended to be very angry at being disturbed but secretly, she liked playing with the children. Sometimes she would even give Harriet a ride, as long as she promised to hold on tight.

Not everyone in the wood was friendly. Vara the viper once lay in wait for the children as they played under the pine tree. Their father saw him hiding in the ferns and ran out in his thick, pine-cone suit with his birch-bark shield to fight the snake.

Tom, Harriet, Sam and Daisy watched and as the battle went first this way, and then that; but at last their father was so quick with his needle-sharp spear that he pinned the viper to the ground. Proudly, the four children picked up the dead snake.

"Where shall we bury him?" they asked.

Just as the children were wondering what to do, an old hedgehog came shuffling up. "I'll take that snake away," he offered with a sly grin. He scuttled off dragging it so fast that the children forgot to ask him where he was going to bury it.

Then Tom and Sam cut hawthorn spears of their own and poked them in the ants' nest. But the ants swarmed out to defend their home and stung the boys until they cried. "Silly boys," said their mother, as she put dock leaf ointment on their stings. "Never hurt the creatures of the forest, unless they mean you harm."

In the middle of the forest is a cave where a troll lives. No one knows his name. One day, when the children were out berrying, Tom saw that the biggest blueberries grew closest to his cave.

"I'm going up there," he said bravely. "And so am I," said Sam and Harriet and Daisy.

"Ho, ho, ho, ho!" said a huge voice, far above them. Berries and baskets tumbled everywhere as the children scrambled back down the slope. They didn't even look back to see who it was. If they had, they would have seen that the old troll of the forest was laughing. It was not often that he had a chance to give someone a fright.

Soon they were in the middle of harvest time and everyone had to do their share. The little brown cupboards in the roots of the pine had to be filled with bottles of berry jam, dried seeds, nuts and fruit to last through the winter. The children's father showed them how to recognize the little pearly-white button mushrooms which would make delicious pies and puddings when the snow was thick on the ground.

Sam did not want to listen and he sat playing with an apple pip, but his father was very angry. "Sam! If you make a mistake, we may all die. You must never pick a mushroom unless you know it is good to eat."

Everyone's hands were sticky with berry juice and the house was full of the smell of newly-picked mushrooms. Harvesting was over, but there was still a lot to do. The fruit must be cleaned and polished, for one rotten berry could spoil the whole crop. Every ripe, brown nut was stored neatly away and each mushroom carefully sliced and threaded so it could be hung up to dry.

The children picked cotton grass and combed it smooth so their mother could spin it into silky thread. Then she would weave it into rugs, or knit pretty creamy-white sweaters for the winter.

*T*he days grew shorter and the moon shone bright and cold as a silver coin, cutting little grey shadows in the pine branches and telling all the forest creatures that summer really was at an end. Mist settled in the hollows like white breath and the children played at leapfrog with the rabbits until it was time for bed.

Sometimes they found forest fairies dancing and singing in the moonlight and joined in their games. "Come back tomorrow night," the children would beg. "Perhaps," laughed the fairies as they slipped away, light as thistledown. There was no telling where or when they would return.

"*T*oday, we are going to see Mrs Owl," said the children's mother. "It's time for you three, Tom, Harriet and Sam, to go to school. Mrs Owl knows more about our plants, trees and flowers than anyone and she will teach you all the ways of the forest."

Tom, Harriet and Sam looked up at the huge, dark eyes of the old owl and felt shy; and for once, they did not say a word.

There were many other animals in school besides Mrs Owl's own three children and some of them, the children knew already. There were two cheeky hedgehogs, two small frogs who had only just stopped being tadpoles, some of the older squirrels, five rather silly rabbits and lots of small birds — chaffinches, tits and jays and even a young woodpecker.

Mrs Owl taught them the language of all that squeaks, swims, flies or runs. She taught them to listen to the message of the wind, and to see the approach of spring even before the first snowdrop. She taught them to keep well-hidden from humans and to be wary of all hunting animals; fox, stoat and dog.

*T*hen came the first winter weather. The wind shrieked through the pines, scattering dead leaves and twigs and sending little animals tumbling to their warm homes. The children's father put up heavy wooden doors to make their home weathertight, as the first white snowflakes began to settle.

Shivering, the children put on thick sweaters and caps and stepped out into the bitter cold. Even the hare had put on his winter coat.

"If only we could sleep right through until spring, like dormice," grumbled Sam, as he helped his mother with the firewood.

Next morning, the sky was a clear, bright blue and the snowy branches glittered in the sun. Shouting with excitement, the children ran outside, stamping in and out of snow drifts and rolling in the snow until they looked like huge snowballs themselves.

The hare was as happy as the children and he raced up, looking for a new game to play. Tom and Sam harnessed him to the sledge and away they went like the wind.

"Harriet! Daisy!" called their father. "We must make up a basket of food from our cupboards. It has been so cold that some of our friends may not have enough to eat."

That evening, sleepy and warm, the children sat round the fire, listening to their father telling stories his father told him when he was a boy, about trolls and fairies, storms and strange cities from long ago.

Winter days, dark and snowy, went by one after another until at last came the first warm breeze. Spring was in the air. Anemones and snowdrops raised their cool white heads and branches became thick and knobby with new buds. Birds began singing and melting ice splashed into every stream.

Everything was rustling and restless, and the children raced about almost mad with excitement.

They paddled and splashed in the stream, damming it to build a water mill. No one cared how wet or muddy they were for no child of the forest can ever catch cold.

*E*veryone in the forest was busy in the bright sunshine. Birds began gathering twigs and moss and soon from every nest and burrow came the cry of newborn creatures. Tom, Harriet, Sam and Daisy were amazed to find that they had a new, round, pink baby brother of their own, too.

A new year was beginning in the forest and this is where we must leave the children. But if you like, think about them and their forest friends, and that way, their story will never end.